Little Owl's Orange Scarf

by Tatyana Feeney

Alfred A. Knopf
New York

Little Owl lived with his
Mommy in a tree house
on the edge of the City Park.

He loved
adding numbers,

eating ice cream,

and riding his scooter.

He usually loved
surprises, but . . .

he did not love his new scarf.

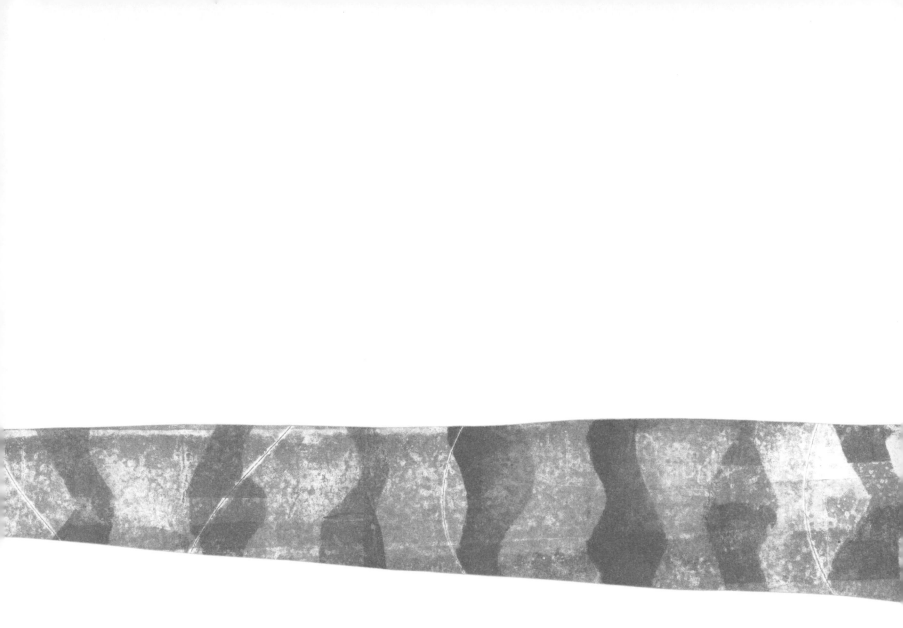

It was itchy.

It was too long.

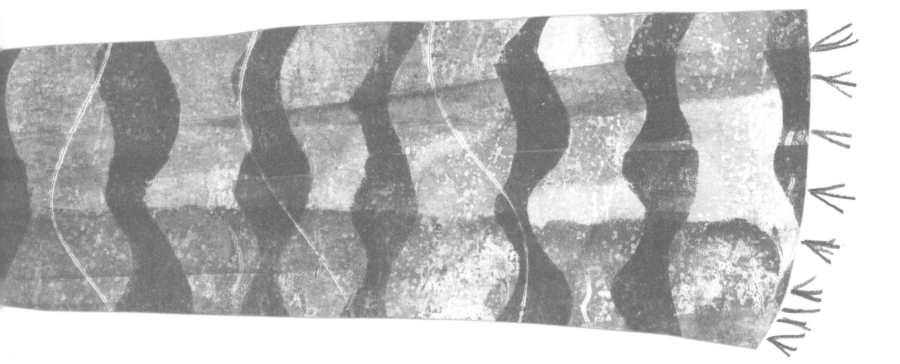

It was far too orange.

"You need to wear your new scarf," said Mommy. "It will keep you nice and warm."

Little Owl tried very hard
to lose his new scarf.

But Mommy always found it.

"You'll need to wear this scarf today," said Mommy. "It's your class visit to the zoo."

Little Owl came home from
the zoo with all sorts of stories.

But Little Owl came home from
the zoo **without** his scarf.

Mommy called the zoo.
Nobody had found Little Owl's scarf.

"Never mind," she said.
"We can make another scarf . . .

and *this* time we will
do it together!"

The yarn shop was more
exciting than Little Owl expected.

After a lot of hard work,
Little Owl's scarf was finished.

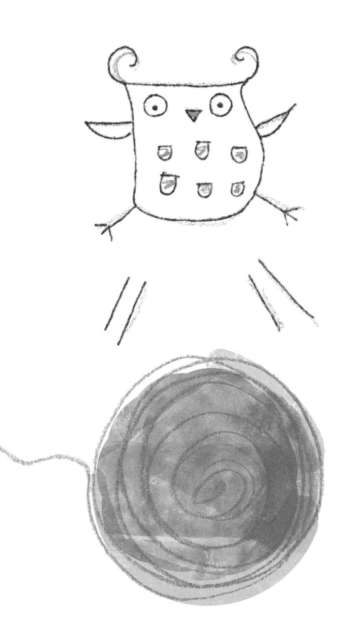

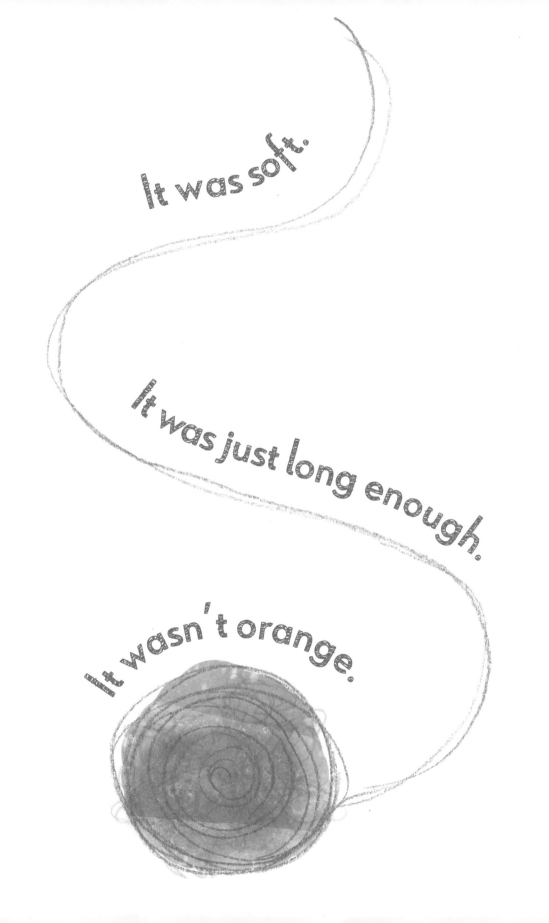

It was soft.

It was just long enough.

It wasn't orange.

Little Owl loved it . . .

. . . especially on visits to the zoo!

THIS IS A BORZOI BOOK PUBLISHED BY ALFRED A. KNOPF

Copyright © 2012 by Tatyana Feeney

All rights reserved. Published in the United States by Alfred A. Knopf,
an imprint of Random House Children's Books, a division of Random House, Inc., New York.
Originally published in 2012 in the United Kingdom by Oxford University Press.

Knopf, Borzoi Books, and the colophon are registered trademarks of Random House, Inc.

Visit us on the Web! randomhouse.com/kids

Educators and librarians, for a variety of teaching tools, visit us at RHTeachersLibrarians.com

Library of Congress Cataloging-in-Publication Data is available upon request.
ISBN 978-0-449-81411-6 (trade) — ISBN 978-0-449-81412-3 (lib. bdg.)

MANUFACTURED IN CHINA
June 2013
10 9 8 7 6 5 4 3 2 1

First U.S. Edition

Random House Children's Books supports the First Amendment and celebrates the right to read.